MW01180761

Arkivestia

By
Emma Philbrick

Peter E. Randall Publisher
Portsmouth, New Hampshire
2021

ISBN: 9781937721787
Library of Congress Control Number: 2021912308

Printed in the United States of America

Peter E. Randall Publisher
Portsmouth, New Hampshire 03801
www.perpublisher.com

Book design: Grace Peirce

THIS BOOK IS DEDICATED TO

Joshua for his love of reading,
Mama and Daddy
for being my amazing parents,
Mrs. Jennifer
for being my co-writer,
Make-A-Wish Foundation
of New Hampshire
for making it all possible,
and Jovi, Emily, and Sasha
for being characters in my book.

Contents

Introduction

In the unknown places in Arkivestia, there is a mysterious creature that brings Austin, Toren, their pets, and their friends on an adventure to the unknown lands of Arkivestia where they make best friends and worst enemies.

CHAPTER 1
Arkivestia

Austin woke up to banging and familiar groans.

Toren what are you doing now? she thought.

Austin quickly dressed in a blue t-shirt and jean shorts. She then brushed her short brown hair and went to see her best friend who had fallen down the ladder again while he was getting his suitcase.

"I wish mom hadn't left," she muttered to herself.

"Toren, we'll be late! You too, Sasha and Asuras."

Soon, they, their fluffy husky Sasha, and their small dinosaur Asuras were packed and ready to ride on the dragon that was coming to pick them up. The dragon had them ride on his back all the way to Arkivestia. Eventually, its wings slowed, and the dragon came in for a landing. It pulled to a stop and dropped off the kids. They looked around and noticed the flat lands of the desert and sandy hills. They made their way toward a mountain and began to climb up when a strange image caught their attention.

"Look!" cried Toren.

Nearby, there was a glimpse of shining gold and black with a white paw.

"It has the tail of a horse . . . " said Toren.

" . . . and the paws of a fox," Austin finished his sentence.

They nodded and ran after it. When they turned the corner, it had already raced by. All they saw before them was a sharp cliff and heavy mist.

Austin and Toren sighed, and slowly walked away, staying far back from the dangerous edge. Austin watched the mist move, swim, twist, and blow around them. But then, it stopped.

Maybe it's just my imagination, she thought. Then, she looked back and noticed it was moving again almost taunting her, *Austin, come find me.* Then like a geyser it erupted and fell back down.

At that point Austin and Toren both decided it was best and safest to head home.

The next morning, bright sunshine filled the windows as Toren woke up to see Austin looking at a picture. He watched her with sleepy brown eyes and ruffled his messy black hair. Climbing out of his bed, Toren shook out his tan pants, stepped into each leg, and put on his red shirt.

"What are you doing up?" he asked, trying to sound wise even though he was the younger of the two. He looked down at the picture in Austin's hands and sucked in his breath. He saw a white paw and a horse-like tail. He stared closely at the picture, and in confusion asked himself, *what is that?*

3

CHAPTER 2

Treasure

During breakfast, Austin and Toren agreed to go exploring. It was their favorite thing to do and they would eagerly head out any chance they had. They ate quickly and ran outside only to find their hiking gear was gone!

"Someone stole it!" Toren groaned.

"Why would someone do that? Everybody has that stuff!" Austin huffed with anger and frustration in her voice.

"I—I don't know," Toren couldn't understand.

Despite their disappointment, the two continued on with their plans. They went exploring out on the hills anyway. The heat of the day quickly set in.

"Ohhh, I'm so hot," Austin groaned.

"Me, too." Toren wiped away the sweat on his forehead.

Sasha was hot too, especially with such heavy fur, but she seemed to smell something. Her nose was twitching close to the ground as she picked up a scent, she began to follow it.

"What's up, girl?" Austin asked. "Do you smell something?"

"Seems like Asuras smells it, too." Toren watched the dog-sized dinosaur sniff the ground in the same way. Their pets dashed off, running away at an alarming pace.

"Hold up, girl!" Austin cried. She and Toren took off behind them, flying through the hot air and right to the edge of the cliff.

"What is this?" Toren was panting with surprise and fatigue.

"Wait a minute," Austin said as she looked around her. "I remember this."

Sasha planted her paws to make herself stop. She turned her neck in the direction of a large rock and began frantically barking.

"Sasha, what's wrong?" Austin asked.

Sasha's barking turned into a whimper. She continued to stare at the rock.

"There must be something in there they want," Toren figured.

"But it's solid rock. How are you supposed to get in there?" Austin looked around. Her eyes widened when Toren pulled out a pickaxe. He raised his arms and took one swing, then . . . holding his pickaxe high in the air, he was shocked at what he was witnessing.

"How?" Toren demanded.

Austin was too breathless to answer. She had seen it, too. The rock Toren had sliced, had ripped apart! They carefully stepped through the open space, waited for their pets to join them, and then heard a suction-like sound behind them. Somehow, the rip along the rock was gone!

"Th-th-this is g-g-giving me the c-c-creeps." Austin's voice stuttered and shook.

"Me too," whispered Toren.

Sasha galloped forward as the two friends walked along the rock. Every new step they took activated a light show above them. Gems along the ceiling of the rock lit up in bright blue and purple. The only thing they could hear was their own footsteps and then, Sasha, who was anxiously barking again. They ran after her, getting further into the strange tunnel, until suddenly, Sasha's paws again dug into the ground. She came to a full stop.

"Sasha . . . " Austin's voice trailed off in amazement. Before her was an open room. They slowly walked inside. There, in one corner was a treasure chest.

"Austin . . . " Toren said softly.

"I know," she answered.

The key was on the floor. Together, they reached for it and slowly walked toward the chest. Toren could feel his heart beating and Austin tried to take deep breaths. With shaky fingers, she inserted the key into a hole near the top of the chest and turned. It clicked open. They looked inside and could never have imagined what they were about to find.

"Our hiking gear!" Austin exclaimed. But there was more.

"Look at all these jewels," Toren added with amazement. The colors gleamed brilliantly.

Suddenly, the room started to rumble.

"Toren, what is that?" Austin cried out.

Toren never had time to answer. At that moment, the ceiling violently shook and then collapsed right on top of them.

CHAPTER 3
Arkivestia's Army

Austin's eyesight was blurred as she slowly started to rise from the rocky wreckage around her.

"Toren!" she yelled with alarm.

A far off *'follow me'* was her only answer. They heard a voice behind them call . . .

"Lunar, we know you are hiding."

Austin and Toren didn't think for a moment what it meant. They took off running but ended up briefly in the arms of two strong men. Then, two figures seized them from behind and brought them to the ground. The pair who saved them wore helmets made of pure gold and silver with lines of red paint on either side. Jetpacks were strapped to their backs and each held a sharp knife. The kids examined what they wore: suits of gold with writing on their shoulder pads. In Arkivestian it bore these markings:

$$\_\ `\sim^/\_$$

Austin and Toren were then swept up into their arms and blasted high into the air, still shocked at how the women took out both strong and muscular men. They zoomed through clouds and above tree-tops, until eventually Austin and Toren could see a wide-open area with a large building in the middle. They noticed a sign on top that read: *Arkivestian's Army*. The jetpacks made a rumbling noise as they lowered them gently down to the ground. The women motioned with their hands for Austin and Toren to move into the build-ing's main entrance. Although both were unsure of what they were doing there, they marched forward and stepped through the door. Looking around at the crowd inside, Austin and Toren stared at dozens of what looked like well-trained men and women wearing the same gold, silver, and red helmets. The room was quiet until a loud voice barked out a command with such sudden force Austin and Toren jumped. They couldn't tell what was happening, only that they needed to move. Along with the crowd, they turned the corner and entered an even larger room with a person inside who seemed to be their leader.

"Are you the Robinses Tribe?" Austin blurted out.

An almost disturbed male voice spoke out.

"No, we are the Arkivestian Army, defenders of Arkivestia and enemy of the Robinses Tribe," the man told them.

Austin and Toren were very puzzled. They looked at each other but soon there was another loud commotion.

"Invaders!" someone cried.

Austin and Toren were quickly taken to another room.

"Put these on!"

The lady pointed to two pairs of old, rugged-looking boots. "They're special," she explained.

"What is so special about these?" Austin asked, thinking they didn't look special at all, just worn and battered.

Toren knew otherwise. He could tell exactly what they were. "They're jet boots controlled by whoever puts them on," he told her proudly.

Austin wasn't convinced. She tugged at them, but the boots wouldn't budge. "I can't move these stupid things!" she cried.

"They are voice controlled," another lady standing nearby told her.

"Yeah, I knew that," Austin retorted, trying not to show her embarrassment.

"Let's go!" Toren yelled.

They watched in amazement as the boots clicked their heels together and the laces flew open. Toren inserted each foot into the gap and stepped his heel flat.

"Tie up," he instructed.

The boots' laces looped together in unison, knotting themselves neatly at the top of Toren's shins. He turned to Austin with a satisfied grin.

"Your turn," he told her.

Austin had no idea how Toren knew what to do, but she repeated the commands.

"Let's go!" she hollered. Sure enough, the boots clicked their heels together and the laces untied right before her eyes. Tentatively, she stepped one foot into the left boot, and then into the right.

"Tie up!" With a whoosh sound, the laces did their looping and a second later finished in a neat knot at the top of each boot.

With a satisfied grin of her own, Austin turned back to Toren and with a firm nod they told the boots to blast off. With a plume of thick white smoke, they, and the members of the Arkivestian Army, were in the air.

CHAPTER 4
The Robenses Tribe

After a flight during which Toren had to carry Austin on his back most of the time because she was asleep, they finally touched down.

Their jet boots landed with a thud on top of the dusty sand.

"Hey, look over there." Austin pointed to another cave. Taking slow steps toward the opening they moved through swirly mist around their knees. Squinting at the walls of the cave, they could see strange markings.

"What do they mean?" Toren wondered.

"Shhh," Austin told him, putting a finger to her lips. "Someone's talking."

They could hear muffled voices. "Let's listen."

The people from the Arkivestian Army seemed to be discussing something quietly over in the corner. A man then turned, looked at the kids, and walked toward them.

"Where do you live?" he asked. He was tall and wore a dark green coat. His serious brown eyes watched them carefully.

"In Jericosia," Austin quickly answered.

"Follow me," he commanded.

Austin and Toren exchanged looks but decided it was best to do as they were told. They walked behind him and began moving swiftly through the shadowy cave, with their pets at their sides.

"Where are we going?" Toren whispered. Austin shook her head. She didn't know either.

A rustle of wind near her thigh alerted her to Sasha's sudden movement.

"Sasha! Where are you going?" Austin sputtered with alarm.

They raced after the sprinting dog, around twisty corners and over rocky dirt to the end of the cave. Sasha barked three times, spun around, and chased her tail.

"What, girl?"

"Austin, look around! We're home!" Toren's face lit up.

Austin exhaled with relief. Sasha knew exactly where the man was leading them! They saw their house again in the distance.

"Thank you," they told the Arkivestian person who had led them home.

It had been an exhausting day.

"Wow, I sure am tired," Austin said in a weary, scratchy voice. She wandered into her bedroom and threw herself onto her bed with a huge yawn. Hoping to slip into a restful slumber, she was back on her feet as chaos broke out.

Crash!

The front door tumbled over, nearly breaking in half. It hit the ground with an enormous thud!

"What's happening?" Toren yelled. They both scurried out of their rooms.

"Who're you!" Austin demanded as two men stepped over the broken door. "What do you want?"

They didn't answer. The kids' eyes went wide with horror as they saw two huge bags hanging over the men's arms.

"Help!" Austin and Toren screamed in unison, but it was too late.

The men threw the bags over their heads. Austin and Toren kicked and fought, but the men were so strong and hauled them away. All they could see inside the bags was darkness. They heard nothing.

The Robinses Tribe had them trapped.

* * *

It felt like many hours later when finally, they were released from the bags. Austin and Toren took huge gulps of fresh air. Austin coughed several times.

"My mouth feels so dry," she told Toren, "and I'm drenched with sweat." She used her hands to brush back strands of her hair stuck to her cheek.

"Me too," he confirmed.

The kids stood up and tested out their legs. Being crunched up in the bags had made their muscles stiff and achy.

"We're in some sort of cell," Austin said, as she examined their surroundings. The floor was made of lumpy dirt and metal bars separated them from a murky-looking hallway.

"They must be the Robinses Tribe," Toren told her. "Look, that's them."

Through the rusty bars, the kids recognized the same two men who had kicked down their front door and taken them away.

"Listen," Austin instructed. "I can hear numbers."

"566233," one of them said in the distance. Austin and Toren forced themselves to concentrate on what they were overhearing, hoping to memorize it.

The man wore a black shirt and pants with many pockets. He paced back and forth while repeating the series of numbers. Then, it sounded like words.

"What did he just say?" Toren asked.

"Let's listen." Austin also thought she heard him mutter more than just numbers.

"That's what it said on the note she dropped."

Austin and Toren stared at each other. "What note?" Austin questioned.

"What note?" Toren repeated.

"Think!" Austin told herself.

She walked to the back of the cell. Pressing her hands on her head, she tried to force her brain to remember.

The man said, the note she dropped. Austin ran that through her head. *Think of a note.* Then, she remembered.

"Ahhh!" she sucked in her breath.

"What?" Toren was desperate to learn.

Austin's eyes went wide on a flashback in her memory.

My number is 566233 call me when you need me.

She could hear it clear as day now. Austin went back into her memory to pull out more. She could hear someone telling her that number, but she still couldn't see who it had been.

"Austin, tell me what you're thinking!" Toren pleaded.

"Hang on," she told him. "Let me think."

My number is 566233. My number is 566233.

Think! Austin let her mind wander back. The number. The voice. Who had told her the number?

A face began to form around the voice. Austin slammed her eyes shut and focused. What had been foggy suddenly cleared. She could see it all!

"That's it!" she said excitedly.

"Tell me!" Toren begged.

Austin's stomach was spinning as she reached deeply into her back pocket for the item she'd carefully hidden away as the guards had searched her for weapons.

She pulled out her phone. Toren's face lit up with hope.

With shaky hands, Austin dialed the number and held her breath waiting for someone to pick up.

"Hello," a soft, happy and familiar voice said in greeting.

Austin's heart leapt. She knew that voice. It was her mother's. With tears in her eyes, she nearly cried out with joy but quickly remembered where she was, and that dangerous people were all around her. She listened to her mother speak again.

"Hello?"

She squeezed her lips together to remain silent. It was too risky to respond. She kept the call on the line anyway.

"It's my mother."

Toren's face went white.

But would Austin ever see her mother again?

CHAPTER 5
Say What?

Austin had shoved her phone back into her pocket, trying to keep it a secret for as long as possible. She and Toren overheard the Robinses Tribe talking about what they would do with them. It all sounded entirely frightening and horrific.

"We could hang them," someone suggested.

Austin shivered. Toren wanted to yell for help but he knew better. He stayed quiet.

Austin knew that there was help on the way, so she kept calm, as her mother was still on the other line. Soon there was a knock on the door. One man asked who it was but there was no answer. Again, he asked. Still, no answer. Austin knew who it was but said nothing.

The man went to the door as two ear-splitting blasts made them jump back against the wall of the cell. The man slumped to the ground. Gunshots rang out!

A tall, strong, battle-ready woman stepped over the man and entered the cell. She wore a bright red and gold helmet.

"Shoot," she said. "Did we miss the party?"

Austin's heart leapt. She knew that voice, it was her mother's! While the soldiers took care of the rest of the Robinses Tribe, Alliea, Austin's mother, quickly untied Austin and Toren.

"Where have you been?" Austin cried; her face soaked with happy tears.

"I don't really know," Alliea told her. "But why don't you come with me and I'll feed you. You two look very hungry."

"That would be nice," Toren agreed, as his stomach rumbled and growled. Austin's mom squinted her eyes as she looked him over.

"Who is this?" she asked her daughter.

"That's Toren," Austin explained. Her mother looked more closely at him.

"What's his middle name?" she inquired.

"Aiden."

"Last name?" Alliea demanded more information.

Austin shook her head. "No one knows," she began. "And why are you asking me this?"

Her mother's face wore a concerned expression.

"He might just be your brother."

Alliea turned away from them and paced back and forth, looking back at the kids several times, as she seemed to be trying to figure something out.

"I thought your father took him to the grave with him," said Alliea

"Say what?!" Austin and Toren cried out in astonishment.

CHAPTER 6

What's the Boy Doing Here?

The friends discovered the truth about their relationship. They were, in fact, brother and sister, and in spite of their surprise, they knew they had to move on to make another big decision.

"Come with me," Alliea told them.

"But where are we going?" Toren wanted to know.

"We're bringing you to meet my boss," she explained.

"Well, umm, ya, do we need to be approved to be in your family?" Toren asked sarcastically.

"No," Alliea told him. "And Toren, didn't you want to join the army?"

"Oh, yeah," he said with embarrassment. "I sort of forgot about that."

They moved out, following Alliea to the place where the Arkivestian Army building stood. The air was thick. Sasha was becoming very annoyed with all the bugs swarming around them, as Asuras wandered over to the mushy banks of a swamp.

Austin and Toren figured that seeing Alliea's boss would be easy because they thought they had met the boss before. But they were very wrong. When Alliea led them through the doors and down a long hallway, they turned into a room and stopped dead in their tracks!

The lady standing in front of them was tall, muscular and stern. She must be the boss. Austin was shocked to see a woman instead of a man.

Toren elbowed Austin. He looked frightened but didn't risk speaking. He kept his mouth shut. They waited for something to happen. Finally, the female boss spoke.

"What's the boy doing here?" she asked. Her voice was sharp and stern.

"That's my son," replied Alliea with a smile.

"Aren't they a little old to join the army?" The woman demanded. "They always start at three, don't you remember?"

"I started at sixteen, remember, Ionel?" Alliea challenged.

Ionel sighed. Both Austin and Toren held their breath as the boss looked them over from head to toe, as if to examine how strong and capable they would be. They both stood very tall and stared straight ahead.

Ionel circled around them.

"Well," she began. "They can start. But, if I don't see progress in the next three days, they're out!"

It was a sharp warning they all heard, loud and clear.

CHAPTER 7
The Camp

"What is this, and what exactly am I doing here?" Austin bellowed.

"It's . . ." Toren started.

"I don't care what it is, just get me out of here!" Austin roared back, cutting him off.

The other teenage Arkivestians stared at her like she had three heads. She shoved her way out of the crowd in embarrassment.

"Hey, you there?"

"Who are you?" Austin demanded to know.

"Emily, and you're gonna need me around," the girl told her. "Who are you?"

"I'm the girl who screamed in the entrance to whatever this is, that's me Austin Bolt."

"Mmm. Well, you better get some sleep because tomorrow we have lunar races and those get crazy."

"Uhh, thanks." Austin said, but wondered what she meant.

Austin watched Sasha doze off into a nap. She looked so quiet and peaceful.

"Hey," another girl said as she came into the room.

"And that's Jovienne. Just call her Jovi," Emily said.

Austin settled down in her tattered bunk bed that she shared with Jovi, and fell into a restful sleep.

* * *

Austin woke up the next morning to the ear-piercing sound.

"What is that?" she shrieked.

"It's the goat horn. Time to get up," Emily told her. "I'm gonna show you around today."

Austin saw huge volleyball courts outside of the girl's bunk. (Which Austin likes to play.) There was a sword training arena and a corral full of . . . horse things!

"Those flying horses, what are they?" Austin mused.

"Lunars, they are a breed between foxes, horses, and pegasi," Emily explained.

The goat horn blew again.

"Lunar races!" Someone cried.

"What . . . " Austin started but she could not finish because Emily already left her in the dust.

"Everyone find your favorite Lunar and saddle up!" The manager cried. Austin's eyes burned, there was so much dust kicked up by the Lunars. She found a tall Lunar and decided she wanted that one.

"Hey, that one is pretty wild."

"Who are you?" Austin said.

"I'm Leo," he told her. "And I'll help you saddle up."

Leo was tall and had a mischievous smile. His eyes were blue, and he wore an orange shirt and jeans.

She was at the starting line in no time and the manager said, "Ready, set, fly."

Austin's Lunar took off with a sudden jolt. They were fifty feet in the air when Lexi, the name she gave her Lunar, decided to kick her off. Austin fell straight through the air and felt a sudden tug on her shirt. Someone had caught her! She was five feet from slamming into the ground and she was saved. But who saved her?

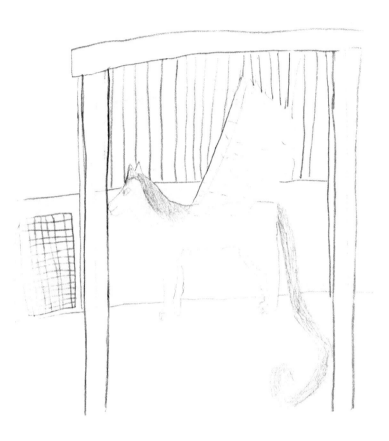

CHAPTER 8

We Meet the Water Lady

Austin was now on the back of Leo's Lunar. *I almost fell, then out of nowhere I'm on a new Lunar! What happened?* Austin felt the strong Lunar touch down on the ground and wait patiently for Austin to get off. Austin got out of her trance and jumped off the Lunar.

"I see you met Leo," Emily said, surprising Austin.

"Oh, yeah, I did," Austin told her.

"Come with me the race is already done," Emily said. "We need to talk."

Austin wondered what she meant but followed her anyway. Emily had taken her to a large mass of water but why?

"Watch." Emily instructed.

Austin stood but nothing happened. Then, suddenly the water burst out into a fountain and created a beautiful young girl. She walked up to Austin and sat by her feet.

> "A prophecy once told in ancient times shall surely come to you,
>> Shall be afraid by a loss
>> But loss shall be fake
>> Says of three girls and one boy running from gates
>> Covered in poisonous vines
>> One girl turns around and opens the gates
>> Only to find six things that shine
>> Three were Arkivestians driven mad and three Fates
>> One man in the middle shall stop them all
>> Only one answer to find."

"What answer?" Austin asked, but *The Water Lady* disappeared.

"That is an ancient prophecy, and she said '*surely come to you*' so that means you will fulfill it." Emily explained.

* * *

Jovi came in and said, "Get in the meeting house right now!" Austin hurried into the meeting house and almost died . . . just like the person on the floor. She tried to see who it was. Then she saw it . . . Toren was lying on the floor . . . motionless.

"He tried to kill an aradose while you weren't here," the doctor told her.

Austin kept remembering the prophecy: *Shall be afraid of a loss but loss shall be fake.* Austin hoped this was the fake loss.

* * *

An hour later Toren was back! Austin was so shocked she almost fainted.

"Austin."

Austin whipped around to see Jovi. She looked worried. Jovi took Austin to an area covered with grass and flowers. She sat down with Jovi and Emily.

41

"Austin, we have to leave, like, right now." Emily said.

"Why?" Austin asked.

"We just do," Jovi forced.

"The guards won't let us pass," Austin reminded them.

"The guards aren't there tonight," Jovi reminded Austin.

The three girls tried to sneak away until they heard a loud, "Hey!"

Austin whipped around and saw Leo.

"Hey," he said again. "I decided to come along."

"Uhh, okay," Austin said though she had no idea how he knew about the midnight breakaway.

They resumed their journey onward.

CHAPTER 9

Everyone Knows a Talking Snake

Austin and her friends got out of the gates without trouble except . . .

"Where are we?" Austin asked.

They looked around the scenery. There were fruit trees and a large shining gold mansion.

"Looks like Heaven to me," Jovi said as she reached for a grape. She was about to bite into it when . . .

"Welcome," something hissed.

"Who or what just said that?" Emily asked in fear.

"Me." The voice belonged to a large scaly fire snake.

"Are you s-s-sorsosnake?" Asked Leo.

"Who's sorsosnake?" Austin asked her friends.

"W-we can't explain," Emily replied.

"It's not like everyone knows a talking snake!" Austin retorted.

Austin heard a slash behind her . . . and then, oddly, she was in chains in some old prison cell. The floors were plastered with bones.

"Where are we?" Austin demanded. "And who is sorsosnake?"

"Well, it's an ordinary snake but is made of fire and has sorcerest powers," Leo said. "And we gotta get out of here or we'll also become a heap of bones."

"Yikes, Leo," Emily said, "where'd you learn so much about him?"

"My grandfather told me tales," Leo responded.

"Shh." Jovi scolded.

As she said this, two soldiers came into the room.

"What's all the noise down here?" a tall man yelled.

"We were discussing something," Austin chimed.

"Discussing what?"

Another man walked into the room. His words were as cold as ice but could burn up your lungs. He had a scar across one eye, which made him blind in that eye, and he wore tall boots. Austin glared at him.

I swear he has spikes on the bottom of those boots, and blood on the spikes, she thought.

"I'll ask again, what were you discussing." He was impatient and looked angry.

CHAPTER 10

The End of the World . . . I Think

A ustin felt dizzy. *Where are we?* she thought.

"Stand up in the presence of the queen, Sorsocolt," the man with the wounded eye declared.

The queen was made out of fire, though she was also a horse.

Sorsocolt, Austin thought, *Who's that?*

Austin was about to find out.

"Take them to the front of the palace. I would like to show them around," Sorsocolt said. "They are guests not prisoners."

She mumbled something to one of her servants that Austin couldn't make out.

Austin and her friends were taken to the front of the palace where there were beautiful gates rimmed with gold and a small door off in the distance.

"What is that door for?" Leo asked.

"I don't know, shall we go see?" Sorsocolt prodded.

They walked over to the door but everything about it was reversed: as you got closer it got smaller, but the door was still big enough to fit two elephants.

"Oh, wait, I remember now," Sorsocolt said. "It was for you. Head in."

"Um, okay," Austin replied, but did not fully trust the queen. She opened the door and walked through the threshold.

Suddenly, Austin and her friends were in a place filled with a smoky mist. A large palace stood before them covered with poisonous vines.

"Austin, the prophecy . . . " Emily said.

"I know," Austin said.

They heard laughter and ran, but then curiosity consumed Austin who whipped back around and, while no one was looking, opened the gates.

CHAPTER 11

The Purple Portal

Inside the gates were Arkivestians and three Fates, bur the man in the middle stopped them from attacing us.

"Get ready to run!" Austin cried.

Suddenly, he morphed into a purple portal!

"I've heard of that, if it gets ahold of you, your whole body disintegrates," Leo warned.

They ran as far as they could, then Austin and her friends huffed and puffed, wearing themselves down.

"Oh, I can't run now. I'm so tired," Jovi coughed.

"Me too," Emily added.

The portal was gaining on them, floating and pulsing as it got closer.

"I have to run after it," Austin cried to her friends.

"But Austin you can't," Jovi warned, "It will kill you you're not strong enough!"

"Austin please," Leo pleaded.

Austin said, "It is the only thing, I have to do this."

Austin felt the heat of the portal as she got closer to it. She ran, gaining speed as she prepared her fingers to release a huge rock. Her hand launched it! Austin watched the rock travel through the air, holding her breath until she knew it hit its target. The rock struck the top of the portal, right where Austin intended, and then everything went black. She knew how to unlock the good power of the portal, she had to destroy the part of it that was powered by blackness and evil.

"Austin, Austin, wake up!" Leo shook her, trying to wake her up.

Austin's eyes flickered open. At first, all she could see were fuzzy images. What had happened? Then, Leo's face appeared above her and she felt his hands shaking her.

"Yeah?" Austin answered, her voice scratchy and weak.

"You're alive!" Leo shouted.

They were all very happy that she was back, but Austin spotted something . . .

"Look! The portal is lit again. We have to check this out!" Austin said, working to rise back up from the ground. "Ouch." Her body hurt everywhere.

She tried to stand up again but failed.

"Woah, woah, Austin, look, don't try to get up yet. You're hurt." Jovi told her, rushing over, "Let's try and find something to bandage your wounds with."

"Look, the other monsters died, the portal must have been their source!" Emily said. Austin hadn't noticed her standing nearby.

They found cloth to wrap around Austin's wounds. As soon as they closed it around her skin, she magically healed. The friends weren't sure how that happened, but they were happy to see Austin standing again. Finally, they were ready to go through the portal. Anxiously, they prepared for what could be a dangerous journey.

"I don't know where this is going to take us, but in we go!" Jovi told the group.

The friends held their breath, and jumped in. They were once again thrown into complete darkness.

They fell onto a strange, marble floor. Looking around, Austin noticed it resembled the Sorsocolt's palace. This time, Sorsocolt was dead.

"She must have been powered by the portal too," Jovi explained.

"Look, another portal." Emily pointed toward a bright splash of light.

"Well, I guess we go in?" Austin said.

"I agree," Leo told her. "Let's do it!"

"Alright. On the count of three. Ready? Three . . . two . . . one!"

In this portal, they were flying alongside shooting stars that brought them to the other end of a rainbow-colored path.

CHAPTER 12
Family Reunion

Austin and her friends fell out of the portal and saw Toren explaining to Ionel when he last saw Austin. Alliea was there listening, too. Then, he stopped dead in his tracks. His eyes went wide with shock.

"Austin!" Toren exclaimed. "You're here!"

"Toren, Mom!" She ran and gave her family a hug. They were so happy to be together again.

Suddenly, a tall man walked in the door.

"Hi, I'm Alex Bolt. Who are you?" he asked them.

"Wait . . . Dad?" Austin stammered.

"W-w-what!" Toren said, "I thought you were dead!"

"Alex, do you remember me?" Alliea said.

"Alliea, is that you?" Alex said.

"Yes, yes, it is," Alliea said.

While the whole family was back together, they felt like all was well with the world, but then . . .

"Alex!" it was Ionel, "I kept you locked up for a reason!"

"You what?"

Me and my favorite dog Sasha.

About the Author

I grew up in New Hampshire and was born in Ohio. I live with my awesome brother Joshua, my amazing parents Elisabeth and Joshua, and of course my favorite dog Sasha. I love the *Origami Yoda* books and a very inspiring book — a book called *Tenny*. I am a big reader and love almost every book and song. My amazing Make-A-Wish New Hampshire family made this all possible. Thank you for reading my book, and I hope you enjoyed it.

Sincerely,
Emma Philbrick